Queenie;
a Novella

Raymond Greiner

To my friend Tom

R. Greiner

pTp
PTP Book Division
Path to Publication Group, Inc.
Arizona

Copyright © 2015 Raymond Greiner
Printed in the United States of America
All Rights Reserved

No part of this book may be used or reproduced by any means, graphic, electronic, or mechanical, including photocopying, recording, taping or by any information storage retrieval system without the written permission of the publisher except in the case of brief quotations embodied in articles and reviews.

Reviewers may quote passages for use in periodicals, newspapers, or broadcasts provided credit is given to *Queenie; a Novella by Raymond Greiner* and PTP Book Division, Path to Publication Group, Inc.

PTP Book Division
Path to Publication Group, Inc.
16201 E. Keymar Dr.
Fountain Hills, AZ 85268
www.pathtopublication.net

ISBN: 978-1516901623
Library of Congress Cataloging Number
LCCN: 2015949470
Printed in the United States of America
First Edition

Dedication

I dedicate my novella, Queenie, to Tom Sheehan the best writer I know and probably will ever know. I sent a submission to Literary Orphans Journal and made a slight mention that submitting to journals at my stage of life is rather inconsistent relating to typical submitters, who are mostly much younger than I am. The Editor-in-Chief, Mike Joyce, wrote me a very long message in opposition to my stated opinion as it related to age as a discrepancy. He went on to tell me about his father, who was his main inspiration, for his becoming a writer and involved in his literary journal. Then, in a broader and more profound statement, Mike told me about Tom Sheehan who was older than I am and his father and has been published in Literary Orphans Journal multiple times and continues to write each day and still submits to many literary journals and magazines. This "crack in the door" opened a profound awakening to me in so many ways. I contacted Tom and he became my mentor and helped me with everything. He taught me many of the things he had learned over his years as a writer. He edited my stories and essays and, from this, I learned much in a very short time. I lack Tom's experience and academic status but he loaned me his mind repeatedly and I cannot express how appreciative I am. I read many of his stories and poems and it astounded me and stimulated me to become a better writer, and I did.

Table of Contents

Chapter 1. War   9

Chapter 2. Alaska   13

Chapter 3. Queenie   12

Chapter 4. Angel   41

Chapter 5. Loss   63

Chapter 6. Moving Forward   67

About the Author

Chapter 1. War

Cold wind and rain is ceaseless and our foxholes have three inches of water soaking our boots causing wonder how our feet will survive if temperatures continue to drop. Bleak, desolate landscape commands visual dominance in every direction. Our company is entrenched in a line of defense connecting with adjacent companies. On the distant hill, we can see our enemy. They mingle about moving artillery in position. Thousands of marshalling Chinese communist troops well equipped and dressed in quilted cold weather garb, preparing for assault. One must question reasons for war. Our goals here I am unable to see or calculate. I only feel despair and anguish. No matter, I must support my comrades and obligated to perform at my best. I am corporal Samuel Williams, responsible for assigned fellow soldiers, and we are facing combat of the highest magnitude. Fear is present, but calmness prevails infused from our training.

The Chinese will come in three waves. Artillery fire directed in front of the advancing troops and also behind the second wave to prevent stalling the advance or spontaneous retreat. The third wave will have no weapons, gathering weapons from scattered dead of the first two waves. These are standard Chinese assault tactics, different from modern American military strategy most often performed by flanking, stealth and ambush.

The battle was intense. US commanders called air strikes and maximized artillery fire. Our M1 rifles became so hot from continuous rapid fire we poured water on the barrels. These Chinese troops were sacrificial, with dead and wounded scattered throughout the plain of attack. There can be no retreat; our only chance of winning this battle is devastation and death of the enemy. Reinforcements arrived and share positions adding firepower, slowing the Chinese offensive. US losses were high and my best buddy was shot through the head and died instantly. The entire scene is indescribable, beyond imagination for those who never experienced the horrors of war. A platoon was assigned to capture enemy survivors to be imprisoned. Our orders then came to pull back to battalion command center for reassignment.

Queenie

Trucks were waiting and we were moved to a central camp with tents in place. After chow, I ventured with my team to our assigned tent and began the process of absorbing all that happened. A resetting of mind and body, as we attempt to cope emotionally. The stench of death haunts us and our minds are scarred deeply by this ineradicable memory. No glory found in war, only agony, death and destructiveness.

How did I get to Korea? Thoughts drifted back. I joined the army in 1951. My childhood and teen years were awful times. There was no love present in any form or dimension. My father was an alcoholic. He physically abused my mother and abandoned her before my memory. We lived with my grandparents and my mother's mental state declined. She eventually was institutionalized. My grandmother was my single source of support since my grandfather was also an alcoholic, not abusive, but unemployed and in a drunken stupor most of the time, babbling incoherent, senseless things. My mother had a brother, Jake, in Alaska who operated a gold claim he staked in 1924. He visited us once when I was twelve years old. I really liked Uncle Jake; he was fun to talk with, told stories about his adventures in Alaska building a cabin on his gold claim on a Yukon River tributary north of Fairbanks. I hated to see Uncle Jake leave. Uncle Jake represented my one and only emotional attachment regarding family love bonding during formative years. Thoughts of him remained vivid.

Even with my dysfunctional childhood, I did fairly well in school and received a partial scholarship to a local small college. I finished two semesters working part time as a busboy, but struggled to hold my head above water financially. I then joined the Army believing it could offer stability, which it did. Now, I am in a raging war, far beyond anything I could have ever imagined. Governments cause wars, and this scenario has been in place in excess of ten thousand years. Soldiers follow like lemmings and die by the thousands to appease government ambitions, supporting politically fabricated goals and agendas posturing to gain power, feathering their own nests and the cost is high. Those Chinese soldiers we slaughtered had families and homes and were trying to live within a system that completely dominated and controlled them. Payment for their service was death.

The reason given for this war was to protect the democracy of South Korea from the onslaught of communism dominant in the north separated by the 38th parallel. The Chinese entered the war to support North Korea creating massive resistance. Finally, the US accomplished a settling point and the 38th parallel was re-established as the boundary of the two conflicting countries and war ceased.

I was at a personal crossroad. I have three months remaining on my enlistment obligation and was transferred to a base in California. Near the end of my enlistment I received a letter from Uncle Jake in Alaska.

Chapter 2. Alaska

"Dear Samuel: I know you are in the Army and have endured the Korean War but since you are my only living relative, of the younger generation, I am reaching out to you for assistance. I am now sixty years old and have been mining my gold claim since 1924 and my body is beginning to feel the effects of aging. Arthritis has set in and getting worse. I can't work the claim anymore and will be going into a care center for the aging and would like you to take over my claim. I can still walk, but must use a cane and am slow. I have 150,000 dollars in a retirement account in Fairbanks and this money should cover my costs during final years. If you come to Alaska, I will accompany you to the claim and teach you all I have learned and also where pockets of gold are most abundant. I also have 25,000 dollars in gold buried on the claim and will give this to you as startup capital. You are in my will and when I die you will inherit the claim. I may live a bit longer, hope to, but we all get old and die and must face that reality. This claim has plenty of gold remaining and it's a lot of physical work during summer to dig and sluice it out, but you are young and I do feel you will enjoy living in Alaska. The cabin is a good one. I built it with great care and planning. It's 30X20 with two rooms and a sleeping loft with a quality cast iron wood burning stove for heat. I also built a cache to store food. I have never enjoyed life as much as I have living at this cabin. It would please me if you accept this offer.

"I can only image what you have experienced in the war and respect you for surviving it. Nothing humankind has done more incorrectly than its habitual attachment to wars. Let me know if you can make it up here. If you need money for travel I will send it. Your friend, Uncle Jake."

I couldn't believe it. I had difficulty sleeping as I thought about Uncle Jake's offer. I will truly be a lost soul when I leave the army, and have no plans or future. I had to take Uncle Jakes offer. I decided to write him.

"Uncle Jake: How nice to get your letter. I have never forgotten your visit when I was twelve years old. I am scheduled for discharge next month and considered re-enlisting but your proposal is a better option. Send me the location where you are staying. I will get a flight to Fairbanks as soon as I am discharged. I have plenty of money to travel, and am looking forward to talking with you again. I can't imagine anything more exciting than this opportunity.

"You probably have a boat and we can travel to the claim offering new direction and I can assist you in any manner I am able. Write soon. Your nephew, Samuel"

A week later, Uncle Jake's response letter arrived.

"Dear Samuel: I was delighted to read you accept my offer. I'm still plenty good to spend time with you at the claim, it will be great fun to show you what I have accomplished during my years mining gold. I love wilderness areas and enjoy studying wildlife. I do have a good boat, with an outboard motor. We can access the claim from Fairbanks in about four hours via river. I had great dog teams over the years, but gave my last team to a friend when my arthritis progressed. I still have the sled, it's a mid-size sled, Ideal for a four to six dog team. You will want to get a dog team, for sure, and can get to Fairbanks for supplies during winter easily in less than a day. It's summer now and I plan to stay with you at the cabin until winter sets in and then will return to the care center. I will teach you the tricks to finding gold. When you get your flight number and arrival time send a letter. I will have my long-time friend Bill Foster drive me to the airport to greet you. Bill worked the adjacent claim for years when he married and his wife Margaret wanted to stay in Fairbanks. He still owns the claim but doesn't work it now. You coming here is the best thing that could happen to us both. I need family connection and support and you need a new direction. You will fall in love with Alaska. Uncle Jake."

I received an honorable discharge from the Army a month later and already had my ticket to Fairbanks and informed Uncle Jake of my flight number and arrival time. I felt so good about this opportunity it seemed like a miracle.

Landing at the airport in Fairbanks didn't seem like Alaska, more like every other city, buildings, traffic and people wandering about. Uncle Jake and his friend Bill were at the gate to greet me.

I hugged Uncle Jake and he introduced me to his long-time friend Bill Foster. He was a tall, muscular man, easily recognized as a one of the North Country, with a very pleasant and comfortable demeanor—much like Uncle Jake.

Uncle Jake said, "How great this is. I am so happy to see you and much lies ahead. We will stay with Bill and Margaret for one night then depart for the claim."

"Sounds good to me. It was a rough road in Korea. I feel fortunate to be alive. Your offer fits perfectly, I need change, and the idea of less people surrounding me is needed while I adjust away from wartime stress."

Bill drove a few miles to his home; a small frame house, neatly maintained and I met Margaret, a very pretty and pleasant woman. Margret made a wonderful meal and I enjoyed Uncle Jake and Bill telling stories of the many years working their gold claims.

Bill said, "It was difficult to give up the claim, but aging was descending and Margaret is the best wife a man could ever find and these issues made me realize it was time for change. I saved over the years and we will be comfortable for our remaining years.

"What I miss most is the beauty of the wilderness and connection with animals and nature. This spectrum of life brings out something unexplainable in a person, may be an ancient genetic reaction."

Uncle Jake agreed, "Oh, yes, unexplainable. The best writers in history have struggled for centuries to describe it. Often use poetry and poetic phrases with flowery words in an attempt to allow readers to feel nature's spirituality. I personally think it's about being there, a personal sensation. Trying to explain it is not only impossible, it's unnecessary. The bliss I feel in wilderness areas dissipates when I return to Fairbanks or other metropolitan zones. Urban areas are foul, raspy places."

I said, "It's interesting to hear this. You two have spent many years in remote, wild places, becoming attached to wilderness areas. When I was in Korea I also was in a wild, remote place and it was, by far, the most miserable time of my life, also unexplainable. I doubt any writer from any era could find poetic, flowery words to describe the horror of it and not only nature's wrath caused misery and sleepless nights; it was mixed with overwhelming fear of dying. Although nature was present, the enemy was also present and introspection in any form was inconceivable. I would have given anything to be in an urban area, no matter how foul or raspy.

"However, I feel a sense of anticipation. War taints everything it touches, there is no beauty when senseless killing trumps all else, and no matter how dysfunctional cities are the battleground makes them look like paradise."

Uncle Jake said, "War is the plague of humanity, pitting human against human, projecting evil, hate and spontaneous killing attached without purpose. In nature, there is no hate, and killing is a necessity only for survival, balance and harmony. You will gain insight and knowledge living in the wilderness, learn about survival and no hordes of Chinese troops will descend upon you. It will be a joyful time for us both."

The next morning Bill drove Uncle Jake and me to a boat dock on the Tanana River. The boat had a 25hp outboard motor and two gas tanks. It was a large, flat bottom boat with a raised, straight bow, designed to carry heavy loads. Uncle Jake explained we would go south on the Tanana about ten miles then take a tributary short cut toward the Yukon River, but won't go quite to the Yukon River since the claim is south of the river. I helped Bill load supplies, Uncle Jake had purchased a few days earlier and, in a short time, we cast off, heading downriver. It was a warm summer day, enhancing the emotion. It was comforting knowing I had an experienced companion. Uncle Jake has lived at his claim for over thirty years and knew every inch of the area, making the trip to Fairbanks hundreds of times.

We turned north toward the Yukon River and in about two hours arrived at Uncle Jake's claim. First sighting was a large wheel device protruding into a wide section of the creek in front of the cabin. Uncle Jake explained this was his fish wheel and used to catch salmon during spawning runs. He dried the fish for his food and to feed his sled dogs, when he had them.

Uncle Jake stiffened during the long sit handling the motor, having difficulty getting out of the boat. I helped him onto the dock. I felt an odd emotional surge, and the cabin was magnificent, not big, but easily recognized as very special, displaying great effort was applied to build this cabin and the entire claim was orderly, emitting a sense of efficiency. There was a utility shed, elevated cache, woodshed and outhouse. Also, a dog kennel and shelter used when Uncle Jake had sled dogs, with various tools hanging just inside the woodshed. The logs used for the cabin's walls were about ten inches in diameter. Green sod covered the roof of the cabin and other building. Moss was used for chinking between logs. This place entranced me.

After Uncle Jake walked a few paces, he loosened up and could move quite effectively using his cane. He smiled, looking directly into my eyes and asked, "What do you think of the place, Samuel?"

"I had not imagined it to be so nice, look so comfortable and is a place I will enjoy to the fullest. The surrounding forest and creek compare to calendar photos of Alaska. No wonder you stayed here for 30 years. I love it."

Uncle Jake replied, "I have so much to tell you about this cabin and the surrounding forest. I built this cabin; cache, woodshed, kennel and outhouse with Bill's help moving logs in place. When one builds a simplistic shelter a penetration forms and the attachment is magnified, greater than when a home is purchased.

"Let's go inside, make coffee and discuss a plan."

The cabin had two rooms, one larger near the front of the cabin, where the woodstove stood, a table with three chairs, sink and work counter for preparing food, pots and pans and metal dishes. Handcrafted pottery coffee cups painted with outdoors scenes completed this room. The back room was storage for clothing to suit various temperature changes, boots, and extra bedding. On a hanger was a fur parka, pants, with large mittens with a cord connecting them to be worn around the neck and mukluks for feet, Uncle Jake's mid-winter clothing. The sleeping loft with ladder access was a low crawl-in arrangement. The cabin had three windows; two in the front room and one in the back room double paned for warmth during winter months. The floor was wood-planked. Also a small two-burner propane stove for use mostly during summer months. Uncle Jake lit the propane stove and began brewing coffee.

Uncle Jake gestured, "Sit at the table. I'll bring coffee. It sure feels good to be here. I can't get this place out of my mind. I have lived here so long and feel despair not being able to function properly to keep the place maintained. I thought of you often and it seemed right you should take it over. You will never enjoy living as much as you will living here."

"Uncle Jake you don't need to go into the care center as long as I am here. You still function quite well, and I can help you when need arises. You are very welcome to stay at this cabin as long as you are able. It makes no sense to me for you not to stay here. I can cut firewood and do the physical work required and you can help in many ways, cook food and we can talk and share life for years to come."

Uncle Jake replied, "It does cause me to think about it. I can't get up the ladder to the sleeping loft. We'd need to build a fold down bunk in the back room. I do feel I can carry some of the load. You were such a good kid when I visited years ago. I could tell you were bright, and now that your army days are over, this is a good path for you. You can earn a good living off this claim; I know this claim inside and out. I don't need money at this stage of life. We can give it a try."

I felt good about this. Uncle Jake knew the wilderness well and all the tricks to manage the rigors of winter. He knew how to find gold and separate the fine gold from black sand. He knew when to sell gold and when to hold it as prices fluctuate. His overall knowledge of living this life was boundless. He showed me his *National Geographic* magazine collection and said I could read these during winter's hibernation. Also displayed a folding bathtub he uses in winter months. His life had meaning and purpose, he read constantly. His back room's bookshelves were filled with subjects of every description. His interest in nature and local animal activity was as important to him as any professional naturalist. He corresponded with the Walter Johnson the long time naturalist at McKinley National Park, a dedicated and knowledgeable scientist of natural land and its inhabitants. They exchanged sightings and results of habitat activity especially wolf and caribou interaction. In such a short time, I learned so much about Uncle Jake, much more than I could have ever anticipated.

Uncle Jake had a stack of rough sawn lumber behind the cabin and the next day we worked together to build his fold down bunk. An extra mattress was in the loft and sleeping bags of various comfort ranges for different seasons.

Uncle Jake offered, "I'll make lunch and show you how to make drop sourdough biscuits. I have a gallon of starter; you can't make it in this country without sourdough starter. It's unheard of."

Uncle Jake seemed happier than earlier, knowing he would be able to remain at his beloved cabin, at least for a while longer. It made me happier too, seeing him in such a state of joy.

We had beans with chunks of moose meat and drop biscuits with moose gravy. It was delicious and we both were hungry. Uncle Jake shoots one moose a year cutting some in strips to be dried.

"Samuel, I hunted game since I was a kid, but in recent years I have come to dislike hunting. There's no joy in killing animals but at this latitude practically nothing grows well because of the very short season, and the permafrost forbids a decent garden. I had to kill animals to feed my dogs; the salmon catch was never enough. Living here one must hunt or starve.

"I need to return to Fairbanks in a few days to retrieve my rifle and other things, and we can buy more supplies. We can stay at Bill and Margaret's they told me I am always welcome. Bill is my best friend, ever."

We stayed a few more days at the cabin organizing things, and Uncle Jake showed me the gold stash he gifted to me. It was buried on the hillside overlooking the cabin, marked with a typical looking stone. He also gave me a general description of where most of the gold can be found on the creek. He uses a pan to discover deposits then applies a wooden rocker sluice box to separate sand and gravel in the general area of the creek where the gold showed in the pan. He also told me about his neighbor who lives down creek about two miles he has known for years and helps him from time to time.

"His name's Philo Ketchum and he's about as opposite as one can be from me and Bill, rather crotchety and not social. Philo is not really as bad as most people think. Mostly he is just inept, and clumsy, doesn't apply himself enough and often makes mistakes from not thinking things through. Combined with his crass personality it portrays him as undesirable to those he contacts. Probably the worst hunter I have ever seen, and struggles to get enough meat for winter. I help him hunt in fall and showed him how to use snare traps for rabbits. He makes it, but barely. His claim is rich with color and he finds many nuggets and he does a good job sluicing. He spends too much on liquor and is often drunk and incoherent. I probably do too much for him, but I can't stand back and watch him die from his own errors. I sort of like him, in an odd sense. He's living out here like the rest of us placer hounds sifting sand to make a living and I feel responsible for him. His cabin is a mess. I have never seen such disarray. He screwed a metal plate to his table and after he eats wipes it with a wet cloth. Makes me sick. You must meet Philo. He's part of the landscape. We'll visit him when we return from Fairbanks."

"Philo sounds like quite a character. When should we leave for town?"

"I think tomorrow is good, and when we return I'll show you how to extract gold from the creek."

"I'm excited about that. Let me operate the motor on the return trip to become accustomed to it and also learn the route better."

"Good idea. We'll leave in the morning."

It was early but the sun was high, one would think it was noon. Daylight this time of year is nearly perpetual. When we arrived at Fairbanks Uncle Jake called Bill from the phone at the fuel dock and he came over right away. We then went to the care center so Uncle Jake could gather his things informing them he would be moving back to his claim and cabin. Bill and I helped carry his personal items to the car, including a large unopened box and two rifles in cases.

As we arrived at Bill and Margaret's, Uncle Jake handed me the box and one rifle in its case. He said, "Samuel, carry these inside I bought a few things you'll need while living at the claim."

Margaret had coffee ready and poured us each cups.

Uncle Jake said, with undisguised pleasure, "Open the box Samuel." Inside the box was a magnificent caribou hide parka, along with pants, mukluks and mittens. "I knew you'd need these for the winter months. It gets to -50 on occasion and you can't function without a fur parka. The new fancy down stuff is not as warm and gets punctured easily then the down leaks out, a real nuisance."

"Thank you, Uncle Jake, so nice. These are very well made. Who made this clothing?"

"Kathryn Manatoo, here in Fairbanks, half Eskimo. She's a master furrier and has made custom parkas for years. She's the best there is at this craft. You won't freeze to death, that's for certain."

I then opened the rifle case and inside was a M1 Garand, the rife I carried in Korea, a .30-06 caliber.

"Uncle Jake, this is amazing, a perfect choice. I know this rifle inside and out. Thanks, so much."

"Samuel, you need this rifle to kill our annual moose and also we have many grizzly bears in the vicinity of the claim. Generally, they are not an issue but rouge grizzlies are in the area, territorial and have no fear of humans. This rifle may save your life. Philo has my .22 we can use for small game. Don't use it much, but Philo needs all the help he can get and that .22 kept him alive last winter."

Bill remarked, "I always wanted an M1 but difficult to find and also expensive. They are the most reliable of all automatic rifles, as you know from your experience in Korea."

Uncle Jake said, "I have a Winchester model 70, 30-06 bolt action, had it for years, a good Alaskan rifle."

The next day Bill drove us to the supermarket and we stocked up on supplies. Uncle Jake also bought a few supplies for Philo. We planned to return the claim tomorrow. During the return trip, I asked Uncle Jake more about Philo, "Does Philo have a boat?"

Uncle Jake replied, "Yes, and a good motor; he goes to town but waits too long and often runs out of things. My not living at the claim makes Philo more vulnerable to his own shortcomings but he also has helped me often, too. Especially when this arthritis set in, he cut and stacked my firewood. After I gave away my dogs, I tried to convince Philo to get a team, to enable him to travel to Fairbanks in winter but he told me he doesn't like dogs. As I thought about it, I was unsure he would be up to the task of managing a team. It's a bit far to walk to Fairbanks in winter but can be done, staying in one of the abandoned relief cabins about half way; I did this a few times—a pretty tough hike. A dog team is a must in my opinion and my team could get me to Fairbanks in about seven hours, really good dogs. The folks in Fairbanks complain about Philo, view him as a degenerate, which he is not. He has a good heart and would help anyone in need. The main complaint is he talks too much when he comes to town, talks to everyone, running on about his life in the wilds. He gets lonely at his cabin, like we all do, and this talking is a form of release. People are generally impatient and have little insight to cabin folks and their lives. Alaska is very beautiful but it's a challenge to live in the bush."

"Uncle Jake, I'll be fine with Philo. I had similar experiences in the army, helping some of the guys who would wander off track. My capitan promoted me to corporal because he liked my flexibility among various personalities and the stresses of combat."

Chapter 3. Queenie

It felt good to get back to the cabin. On the door was a note from Philo saying he needed to talk with Uncle Jake. We took the boat to Philo's cabin and he lingered outside. We sat on a bench in front of his place and Uncle Jake introduced me to Philo. He seemed happy to meet me and knew I was a Korean War veteran.

He spoke to Uncle Jake, "Jake, two guys came down the creek in a boat. They identified themselves as government bounty hunters and wanted to kill wolves. They told me a wolf pack lived in the vicinity and wanted to know if I knew where they could find their den. I know how attached you are to wolves. I didn't mention the pack that lives over the hill that you study from time to time. I wanted you to know about these two."

"Thanks Philo, glad you didn't mention our resident pack. I've been corresponding with the McKinley Park naturalist. He presented a long and detailed paper to the government, revealing his ten-year study of wolf/caribou relationships. His study revealed wolves are doing no damage to caribou herds and the bounty should be lifted. I'm hoping this happens soon. These wolves are critical to the balance of things, including caribou, and we need to stop killing them."

"I knew this would be important to you, and didn't mention the pack because I knew that's what you'd want."

"What these bounty hunters do is lay a carcass out to bait the wolves then shoot them when they approach the bait. We could lose the entire pack. Also, Samuel and I brought you a few supplies from Fairbanks to help you out."

"Thanks Jake, I'm getting low on some things. I need to take my boat to Fairbanks soon."

We motored back to Uncle Jake's cabin. Philo seemed okay to me, he was not as adept at this life as Uncle Jake but has lived in his self-built cabin for five years working his gold claim and this is a respectable achievement. His cabin is not as nice as Uncle Jake's but sufficient and it's probably the best he could do.

Uncle Jake said, "Samuel, I can't make the hike over the hill to check on the wolf pack, but will give you a good map and tomorrow you can do it. I have a good lookout spot I will show you on the map and, with binoculars, you can take a look and tell me what you see. These wolves are like family to me. I've seen many cubs come and go over the years. They are very social animals and work as a team at everything they do. I also kept a diary of my observations and sent this to Johnson, the McKinley naturalist, to add to his study program."

"OK, Uncle Jake, I'll do my best."

The next morning I hiked to the ridge and found the lookout spot Uncle Jake described, using the map he sketched. I found the den but no wolves were in sight. Uncle Jake told me there was a pack of eight. I waited all morning and still no wolves showed up. Then I returned to tell Uncle Jake.

"Uncle Jake, I found the den but no wolves."

Uncle Jake offered, "They should have returned by now. They usually hunt at night. From Philo's description, these bounty hunters seem to know what they're doing and may have used strychnine-laced meat as bait. They could have poisoned the entire pack. I don't think they would be able to shoot them all. You can return in the morning and, if they're not there, it's a bad sign. If no pack is present, you'll have to crawl into the den. It's my guess you'll find a litter of cubs; it's the time of year for their birth. If cubs are in the den it is likely they are still nursing or you would have seen them wandering about. I have a turkey basting tube with rubber suction ball and powdered milk you can mix with water to feed them if any are present."

"OK, Uncle Jake, it's still daylight. I'll get the milk and basting tube and head back to the den."

Uncle Jake emphasized, "I am almost positive you will find a litter. Take my pack basket, and a gallon of water to mix the powdered milk. Take your M1, too, just in case a grizzly smells them and tries to get at them."

I was excited to see if Uncle Jake was right. I climbed the hill and made it to my lookout; still no wolves in sight. Walking slowly to the den, dug out under a large boulder, I crawled in using my flashlight. There they were, six of them, staring at me. They did not seem frightened but whined a little. I picked each one up and looked them over one at a time and they seemed in pretty good shape, staring intently at me with their penetrating eyes.

I mixed the powdered milk with the gallon of water, using the basting tube to feed each cub. They were extremely hungry. I kept moving from one to the other and, in a short time, the entire gallon of milk was gone. They were re-energized almost immediately and began playing and biting at each other. One came over and started chewing lightly on my hand. This was such an amazing experience. It's likely the bounty hunters poisoned their parents and siblings, and these were the survivors. I was their savior. I have never felt such instant bonding, overwhelmed with desire to make a life for these beautiful critters of the wilderness. Uncle Jake loved wolves and was mesmerized by their ability to survive, showing close social connection and loyalty. I share his emotions highlighted by this extraordinary moment.

They were small enough I could put four in my pack basket, slung my M1 and carried the remaining two. I stopped about half way to the cabin and let them run around for a few minutes, then packed them up again and made it to the cabin. Uncle Jake came out with a smile on his face. He exclaimed, "I just felt it, knew there would be a litter. Six of them, I love wolves. Well, Samuel, here is your team; the best sled dogs on earth are harness-trained wolves. They are bigger, stronger and smarter. Their feet are tougher and just overall better. Two of Alaska's most prominent mushers, the Markham brothers, took their team of wolves across the entire state of Alaska in the winter of 1930. They were amazed at durability of the wolves and, especially, how their footpads held up, using booties only a few times. Many great sled dogs are crossbred wolves, usually half or quarter. It's difficult to find enough wolves for a full team. You are extremely fortunate to be given this opportunity. They are very young, important for their adaptation to humans. The timing is right, if they were a few weeks older, they would be fearful of you, but now they will do the opposite, they will imprint, the same as if you were one of their parents. It will be great fun to see this happening.

"Samuel, you now have two jobs, working the claim and feeding these hungry wolves. They will need a lot of meat and, also, dried salmon. I have 100 pounds of dried salmon in the cache but they will go through that fast after they are weaned off the milk, which will be soon. We need to start hunting as soon as they begin eating meat. Can't hunt large game now, too warm, the meat'll spoil. Maybe a few rabbits, they will eat those in one day. Next trip to town we will buy two hundred pounds of dry dog food but use it only if we have no meat. The kennel is in good shape and the shelter is adequate for all six. I'm so glad I kept my kennel; also, I have six harnesses and sets of booties for six dogs. This winter we'll begin training. It looks like I'll be with you all winter. With a bit of help, I can make it okay, and you need me to help train your team."

"Uncle Jake, you should stay as long as you possibly can. You won't need much help, you just move a little slower now. I'm the one that needs help, not your body, but your mind. It's a good fit. We can make it work."

I put the litter in the kennel with a water bucket. They seemed confused, so I went into the kennel with them and they stayed right next to me, just as Uncle Jake said they would. They were so beautiful and perfect. I'm as Uncle Jake said, "extremely fortunate" and I knew it.

I walked to Philo's cabin to give him the news about the wolf cubs. He seemed somewhat curious but said, "I never cared too much for dogs and wolves may eventually be dangerous. I'll hike back with you and take a look."

As Philo and I approached the kennel the six rescued wolf cubs began to whine and put their feet on the kennel wall. Philo didn't say a word just stared at the six cubs. I asked Philo to come inside the kennel so the cubs could get to know him.

He was hesitant but walked in behind me. The smallest one, and the only female, came over to Philo and put her paw on his boot, looking directly into his eyes. Philo looked at me with a puzzled expression.

"Philo, I think she likes you."

He smiled, and then patted the cub's head. This was the beginning of a transition for Philo. This girl was a charmer, if there ever was one.

Uncle Jake came out of the cabin and greeted Philo.

"Hey, Philo, glad you came over, these wolves are magnificent. They will seem a little confused for a while but, shortly, they'll have completed their bond. Because they met Samuel at their den, he will become their Alpha and you and I are fellow pack members. They will establish an omega wolf representing the lowest position of the pack. In some ways, the omega wolf is as important as the alpha, completing the pack's structure. Omegas are not shunned but represent a position; although usually eat last. Alphas and omegas form bookends, so to speak. Pack order is essential and the few mushers who have experienced all wolf sled teams believe this behavior is a reason they are so efficient pulling sleds, forming harmonious strength and bonding at a higher level than typical huskies.

"We humans are intruders but these cubs don't feel intrusion. They view us as important members of their pack and our interaction with them will enhance our lives and theirs. I feel blessed to participate in their development and will enjoy watching them transit their lives as our companions."

I could sense a change in Philo as we all were facing a life changing experience with these six wolves. Uncle Jake and I were compassionate toward wild animals. Philo appeared smitten by the female and she with him. An interesting observations as Philo is much like me, love has been absent and these amazing critters have touched our hearts. Uncle Jake included. Uncle Jake almost married once but lost out to a debonair guy that swept away the love of his life. So, here we are, three lonely men and this new family has rescued us as we rescued them. Don't we all need rescuing at various stages of life?

Uncle Jake suggested, "I think we should work our claims in the mornings then the remainder of the day hunt small game. Philo can help if he wants. These cubs need food and lots of it, especially at this early stage. I will set snare traps for rabbits and Samuel can use my .410 gauge shotgun and Philo has my .22. This should work out. My stash of dried salmon will last awhile, but next week Samuel and I will take the boat to Fairbanks and buy two hundred pounds of dry dog food to supplement what we kill. After frost sets in, we will hunt whatever we can, caribou, moose, grizzly bear, all can be cut up and stored in the cache. Also I will activate the salmon wheel during the spawning run. Much work ahead, and with the first significant snowfall, we'll begin introducing our wolves to harness and sled, gradually. I'm experienced at this and will guide every step. Wolves are smarter than dogs and these wolves likely will keep more dog like temperaments because we found them early."

Philo said, "I will help. I can hunt rabbits for the wolf cubs."

Uncle Jake smiled and said, "Good Philo, we need all the help we can get. We will begin our routine tomorrow. Philo, you can meet us here each evening and we will share a meal and discuss progress.

"Samuel, your task is to name each cub. They must begin to learn their names as soon as possible. It's important when they begin sled training."

"OK, Uncle Jake, I'll give it try."

I couldn't stop staring at the cubs; they seemed perfect life forms, alert to every movement and noise. I put my hand through the kennel fence and they smelled it then licked my hand looking at me with their penetrating eyes. They were so beautiful, pure and innocent, blessed with high sensory abilities and instincts, far above human senses. When we think sensory ability we relate to physical senses, such as smell, sight and hearing, but through the centuries stories of wolf interactions have displayed ability beyond physical sensory abilities, revealing spiritual connective consciousness between pack members, be they wolf or human. This is a fascination and I must be alert to these potential interactions.

No immediate thoughts appeared of name selection for these six. I must think about this, maybe in Uncle Jake's *National Geographic* collection I can find animal name suggestions or could discover clues observing each wolf's behavior, which may show specific identifying traits. One male's coat is very dark but with many white flecks in contrast. The female displays signs of leadership. When I approach the kennel she is always first to greet me, then the others follow. This task will be a challenge but Uncle Jake is right; they must have individual identities important to training and teamwork.

The next day we began our new routine, digging in the creek and sifting sand and gravel in our sluice box. Uncle Jake used these hours to make snare traps to catch rabbits for our cubs. His job would mostly involve trapping rabbits. Digging in the creek was too much for him but, using a walking staff, he could move quite well to various places to set his traps. I hunted in the afternoon with the .410 and Philo did the same in the vicinity of his claim, using his .22.

Around 6 o'clock in the evening, Philo showed up with three rabbits and I had killed three. Uncle Jake's traps would be effective after dark and he'd check them in the morning. We dressed the rabbits and cut the meat into small pieces to feed our hungry cubs. We continued to give them milk, which they now were lapping.

Queenie

Uncle Jake assigned himself resident cook and made a great meal of rice and salmon with sour dough biscuits and honey. He enjoyed cooking, a blessing for the three of us.

During dinner Uncle Jake asked, "Samuel, how are name selections coming along?"

"Not too well, but I'm working on it. One male I'll be call Flecks, because his dark coat is covered with flecks of white. The female is definitely the leader; she's extremely alert to everything and is the queen of the pack. I will name her Queenie, it's befitting. Another male shows a peculiarity, when he hears various sounds his ears rotate side to side, the only one of the six that does this. His name will be Radar. I'm stuck for the remaining three and am studying your *National Geographic* magazine collection to help with the last three name selections. Do either of you have any ideas?"

Philo said, "I can't think of any but you are right about Queenie. I, too, noticed her leadership qualities."

Uncle Jake said, "*National Geographic* has many articles on animals; it may be a good source.

"I have spent much time studying wolf behavior, stayed a week at McKinley Park, working with the Johnson brothers, the park naturalists, and they know more than anyone on the planet about wolf behavior. I also communicated with them by letter, relating my experiences. More often than not, the Alpha female leads hunts and is usually a more skilled hunter than the males. Also, the best dog teams usually have female lead dogs.

It's not necessary for the lead dog on a sled team to be the largest or strongest but must it be the smartest. So, it's my guess Queenie will be the lead wolf on your sled team. What gets the Johnson's attention is how these wolf packs know exactly what to do and when, as if they communicate telepathically. I have noticed this also in my studies.

"When the pack hones in on a caribou herd they assign runner wolves and killer wolves. The runner wolves are the youngest. Caribou can outrun a wolf, so they resort to tactics. The runners chase the caribou herd back and forth to wear them down but also for another reason. As these runners are chasing the herd, the killer wolves study the caribou intently, identifying which caribou display signs of fatigue, dropping back.

"The Johnson brothers have studied many carcasses of wolf-killed caribou and almost every time it is an aging or sick animal. Young caribou can run as fast as the mature animals after only a few weeks of life. When the killer wolves make their choices, they attack on the oblique, intercepting their prey, who are faster, also allowing them to strike at the caribou's side with full force, knocking the prey down then several wolves make the kill.

"The Johnson brothers have proven beyond doubt that wolves are in no way responsible for the recent caribou herd diminishing, as was assumed; thus, came bounty on the wolves. The decline was strictly to do with a higher human occupation of caribou habitat, and natives were even given rifles by the government to kill caribou for clothing and food. They killed them by the hundreds. Caribou and wolves have been interacting for thousands of years without major loss of herd numbers. Only fifty years ago caribou herds numbered in the millions. Wolf intrusion on caribou is essential for herd natural management. Wolves need caribou and caribou need wolves. It's nature personified, as seen in all earthly natural functions, it's about balance and harmony, yielding longevity for both species."

I said, "Uncle Jake, I am impressed at your knowledge of wolf behavior. This will become valuable from here on as we move forward with our six beauties. They do amaze me, and they are still very young and inexperienced but I can sense and see from their early behavior they are much different than typical dogs. I'm in great need of your help, Uncle Jake. What would I do if you were back in that horrid care center?"

Uncle Jake responded, "I am so grateful you decided to come to Alaska. It may have saved my life and definitely will make my life better during my time remaining. You have the vigor of youth and your war experiences toughened you beyond what a typical civilian job could ever do. The Korean War had two enemies, one being the weather. Probably worse than Alaska, considering you were poorly equipped for cold temperatures in Korea. Here you will not freeze because you will have the best of the best clothing and you can always build a campfire. It's my bet you'll learn to love Alaska as much as I do."

I searched Uncle Jake's *National Geographic* collection for appropriate names for the three remaining wolves, studied their behavior for a hint of some feature that may relate to name selection. All six were intense, regarding thought and concentration, displaying curiosity. They studied things, listened and watched every movement we made, trying to relate and understand. Wolves rely on natural intelligence for survival, a built in characteristic. Queenie may be a bit quicker mentally but all six were far above typical dog intelligence. I spent time with them outside the kennel each day, played with them. They enjoyed this. Uncle Jake told me it's common to chain sled dogs and few ever offer shelter to their dogs. He never chained his dogs and spent quantities of time interacting with them, built the kennel to allow them a sense of having a den so they could huddle out of the cold wind of arctic winters. He would even bring them into the cabin when temperatures dropped to extremes. He believed personal bonding with each of his sled dogs was a critical issue to gain the maximum from them and, also, him. I feel the same.

One wolf displayed comic traits, always biting at Queenie trying to get her to play, usually with success because Queenie also had a similar spark for playfulness. It was pleasurable to watch these two interact; they would do their circle run game, stop abruptly, stare at each other briefly then off again. The other four males were spectators, entertained by these spontaneous outbursts. I decided to call this zany boy Jester. So, I had Queenie, Flecks, Radar and Jester.

    This time of year in Alaska there is mostly sunlight, only a few hours of darkness and then not too dark. On a few nights, the moon was fairly visible and, on those nights, one of the unnamed wolves howled, only him, and soon the moon disappeared and he stopped howling. It hit me that this guy is a moon howler and, eventually, when the moon is visible for longer periods, he will direct a chorus as the other five join in. I will call him Luna. It fits him well. One cub remained unnamed, and no clues for this guy yet. I watched him each day for some sign relating to his unique behavior, but nothing came to light. All six wolves were beautiful and smart. This, yet to be named, wolf showed a mix of traits, playful but not as playful as Jester and probably second to Queenie in intelligence. He had the longest legs and it could be predicted he would likely be the fastest runner, but they were too young to test this theory. He didn't have flecks and his ears did not rotate, nothing stood out. I decided to call him Incognito, may change it or may not. He needed a name too for his own identity and now he has one. The pack now all had names, Queenie, Flecks, Radar, Jester, Luna and Incognito. Uncle Jake got a real kick out of my name selection, especially Incognito, making him laugh. Queenie was the queen and she knew it, as did the rest of we pack members. We three human members began using their names frequently in daily interaction with our wolf companions and soon they began to respond.

Uncle Jake observed, "I can immediately see these lobo pups are far above typical huskies. They sense and respond to commands more quickly and at such young age. This is going to be great fun.

"The males will be stronger than Queenie; larger and powerful pulling dogs, called 'wheel dogs'. Queenie will be our up-front brains, the leader, and I'm betting on this girl. She amazes me already. You can see it in her eyes, her movements and general temperament displaying one of a leader. What a beauty she is."

The cubs were growing fast and they enjoyed each day playing together, jumping on their human pack members and licking faces, delighted with their lives. Uncle Jake's snares produced the most meat but Philo was becoming a skilled rabbit hunter and brought at least four each day. The game we provided, plus Uncle Jake's salmon stash was holding well but I decided to go to Fairbanks and leave Uncle Jake and Philo to care for our wolf pack. I wanted to make sure we had enough food for our future sled wolves.

I made the trip and stayed at Bill and Margaret's one night and told them about our wolf project. They were thrilled and Bill had known a musher in previous years that had an all wolf sled team, and the old musher said they outperformed any dog team he ever had.

Queenie

Bill drove me to the store to buy dog food and other supplies. We loaded everything the next morning and I was off again on the river heading back to the claim. On the return trip the hum of the motor and the spectacle of the forests stirred thoughts about all that has happened, as I pondered the future. I felt good on the river, moving along with the motorboat—such a contrast to the Korean War.

As I arrived at the claim, Uncle Jake had the wolves out and they greeted me at the dock. Yelping and jumping around with much tail wagging. I patted their heads calling each by name.

We put them back in their kennel, except for Queenie. I unloaded the boat and put the dog food in the cache. I had to pack a load of things for Philo that I'd purchased for him in Fairbanks and took Queenie along. This girl was a delight to be with and Philo was crazy about her.

When we arrived at Philo's claim, he was sifting gravel in his sluice box. Queenie saw him and ran toward him, jumping on him wagging her tail and whining. Philo smiled and greeted Queenie. I took things inside for Philo and he offered me coffee then we sat and talked. Queenie sat next to Philo, with her paw on his foot. These two were intensely bonded.

"Philo, why don't you keep Queenie here for a few days, she is so attached to you. It would be good for you both."

"Sure, I'll enjoy her company, she's really special, the smartest of the pack."

Queenie seemed to know the plan, sat next to Philo and I walked back to my claim. I feel this will be a long-term arrangement for Philo and Queenie, a great companion for Philo.

The routine continued. Philo showed up each evening with a few rabbits. Queenie and we enjoyed this time discussing things. Queenie stayed in the cabin with us, sitting near Philo. Uncle Jake's traps were filled each morning and food was holding up well. The salmon would start running soon and Uncle Jake would activate the salmon wheel to gather spawning salmon. We'd sun dry salmon steaks on racks with salt for preservation, storing the dried salmon in our cache.

When cold weather arrives, Philo and I will hunt any big game we can find. I will use my M1 rifle and Philo will use Uncle Jakes Model 70 Winchester. Moose is preferred as the best tasting and caribou and grizzly bear are also in the vicinity. I don't enjoy killing animals and can't imagine doing it for sport. Living here in this wild place, with six wolves to feed, plus three human pack members, I have no choice and will approach this task with this philosophy.

I walked back with Philo and Queenie. He said he wanted to show me something. Queenie went into the cabin ahead of us and plopped down in the middle of the floor, thumping her tail. Philo's cabin had no resemblance of the mess it was previously; everything in perfect order and the steel plate screwed to the table was gone. Philo's clothes were hung and neatly arranged.

I asked, "What happened Philo? Your place has made a complete transition."

Philo responded, "I decided, with Queenie here, it seemed right to straighten things up. She seems to like it better, makes me feel better too. I sure do enjoy having her with me. She listens to everything I say. I also have not had a drink since Queenie arrived. Don't crave it anymore."

"It looks really nice, Philo. Queenie is a positive element in your life and in all our lives."

The wolves were growing, not mature, but soon would be. I'm looking forward to working with Uncle Jake to train them to harness and sled. We continued to dry and preserve salmon and a slight chill filled the air. I worked the claim each day for a few hours and found several pockets of glitter and a few nuggets. Philo did the same; he was a diligent placer miner. Each day was filled, feeding wolves, hunting rabbits, drying salmon and sluicing gravel. We looked forward to our evening meal and Uncle Jake was an excellent cook, making him feel like a contributor to our effort. Philo and I appreciated and admired Uncle Jake; he was our mentor, guide and knew all the nuances for living in this place. He also loved those wolves.

The first snowfall was light and temperatures stalled placer mining. Queenie and Philo continued to hunt rabbits and we gathered each evening to discuss wolf sled training.

Uncle Jake said, "We'll wait until the snow accumulates but temperatures are low enough to store fresh meat and we can begin hunting for the winter food supply. We're in the caribou annual migration pathway but no way to predict when they'll show up. When they do, we will select four to kill and must butcher and transport the quarter sections as quickly as possible, not leaving the carcass overnight, keeping predators out of the area. I don't know of any active wolf packs nearby but their hunting range can extend one hundred miles. It's best to butcher quickly and get the meat cached. I'm hoping our wolves will be trained to harness enough to transport kills."

Another week passed and snow was now a few inches deep. Following Uncle Jake's instructions, we began sled training our wolves.

Uncle Jake proposed, "The team is large enough now to begin step-by-step training to harness and sled. Each day for the next three days we'll harness the wolves in position, let them become accustom to their harnesses, remaining stationary for about 15 minutes. This gives the team familiarity with the harness. Their learning curve and speed of adjustment depends on Queenie. We will use a two-leader dog system with Incognito as co-leader and Queenie on the left, the position of control. She will make initial moves and directional changes. Incognito is a close second to Queenie in intelligence and also the fastest and he will help set the pace. The rest of the team will recognize her as a leader, watching her, gauging how she reacts to the training and emulate her. This will carry forth for as long as they are a team. When she turns, they turn, when she stops, they stop. It is quite fascinating to watch how they adapt and respond. Wolves make perfect sled dogs; their instinct is to work as a team, exactly as they do in the wild."

We did as instructed and the wolves seemed excited, sensing this was something important. Queenie knew she was the center of attention, wagging her tail when she saw the harnesses come out. By the third day, all the wolves became exuberant seeing harnesses.

Uncle Jake said directly, "Samuel, hand lead Queenie walking her slowly to get a feel for the weight of the sled. It's empty and light, I believe she will respond instantly, and the others will follow her lead."

I did as Uncle Jake instructed and he was correct. Queenie pulled that sled without hesitation. She knew exactly what to do and her harness mate, Incognito, and the remainder of the team responded. After a few yards, I stopped and petted Queenie and Incognito and congratulated the team. They all looked at me with ears up.

Uncle Jake spoke with pride, saying, "It's so fabulous, I knew Queenie would respond instantly and she did. Keep repeating this for about an hour. We will repeat the walking drill for three days and then test them on their own. The first test day we will move in a straight line.

Samuel will walk just ahead of the team. The command to go is 'mush' and to stop 'whoa'. The command for left turn is 'gee' and right turn is 'haw' and to make a 180-degree turn the command is 'come gee' or 'come haw'. These same commands are used for plow horses. Samuel will then hand turn Queenie while giving direction commands.

"After a few days of this procedure the next step will be Samuel standing on the rear runners in the driver's position and Philo, walking slowly in front of the team; allowing the team to adjust to the added weight. Also, giving commands to go, stop, and turn left and right and also to turn 180 degrees."

Philo and I worked together and it was a most interesting experience. The wolves changed demeanor in an interesting manner. They all were playful and, from this, I expected less concentration. Quite the opposite, they became dedicated students. You could easily see this occurring as naturalists have observed while studying wolves. They observed a perceived telepathic sensory perception coming over the wolves, a desire to become involved; maybe, a similar reaction during early hunting experiences, following leader wolves and emulating them. The lightheartedness disappeared during training sessions. This was no surprise to Uncle Jake.

He told us, "They're more intelligent than typical sled dogs, pick up on what's happening much faster, as you readily observe. We have an extraordinary team here and they'll soon prove me correct."

Queenie

Each day, we made progress and were nearing a final test, involving me only on the rear runners, without Philo in the lead. We were on our own. Because they had yet to increase pace, run fast, I was unsure what they would do when I coaxed them run faster. Uncle Jake advised me the command to run is "mush, hike, hike, hike," spoken rapidly and he offered, "They will get the message immediately." I did just that as we entered a long flat section of the trail. Queenie ignited like a rocket, Incognito, liking nothing better than to run, shifted into high gear, and off we went. I couldn't believe it, we were flying down the trail and I felt uneasy about the speed and commanded, "Whoa!" Queenie slammed on the brakes. It was the most thrilling experience I have ever had as Queenie glanced back at me, wagging her tail. Uncle Jake hit this one dead center. We have a great sled team of fabulous wolves. I wondered where this would lead us. It will be great fun finding out. I commanded mush, "Come gee" and we headed back to Philo and Uncle Jake, two old guys meeting us with smiling faces. "Whoa" and Queenie stopped directly in front of Philo, whining.

Uncle Jake said, "I told you so. They are magnificent, I have never seen the likes of these wolves in my life."

The next day, our routine changed. Philo and I hunted early in the day for any game we could find. We killed a cow moose and butchered her where she fell. We then returned for our sled team and they performed flawlessly on their first freight-hauling task. We stashed the meat in the cache and hoped to add more over the next few weeks. Winter was approaching and as Uncle Jake told us often, it will be too cold or stormy for hunting, so we must get all the game we can as soon as we can. This became the priority mission.

We also cut and stacked firewood for both cabins. Hunting and preparation for winter consumed our days. I was now using my skin parka when I took the sled team out; it worked perfectly, with the fur pants, mukluks and mittens. Temperatures were running around zero degrees during days and fell lower at night. Darkness now dominated, allowing only a few hours of daylight for hunting. A small herd of caribou came through on their migration and we killed four as planned. Philo observed a large male moose wandering along the creek and we both went to the area of the sighting and found him walking along the river. I shot him and he fell near the bank of the creek. I went back to get the team and Philo began butchering. We worked together to get quarter sections cached, and our stockpile increased. Philo continued to hunt rabbits, keeping our cache stores intact for later, when winter comes down hard.

Chapter 4 Angel

I assumed Uncle Jake's rabbit trap line. Winter offers the most mental challenges to those living in arctic zones. I planned to read Uncle Jake's *National Geographic* magazines and he had a short wave radio that picked up Fairbanks AM and FM stations. At scheduled times, one station broadcasts news relating to those living in the surrounding isolated regions ... trappers, prospectors and claim owners scattered all over usually on rivers or creeks. We became acquainted with them through these broadcasts, although likely will never meet them in person, unless on a chance trip to Fairbanks. One of the programs spoke of a woman who lived alone in a cabin on the Tanana River. She was born and raised in the cabin her parents built in 1935. Her father was a fur trapper his entire life and taught his daughter every trick in the book, teaching her to run his 100-mile trap line. She began riding the sled when she was 12 and at 15 had her own team of huskies and developed her own trap line, which ran north 80 miles. It took two days to check her traps and harvest beaver, mink, fox and muskrat, staying overnight in a tent with a small wood stove. She would bring two or three dogs into the tent each night. Often it was -50 degrees. In a letter written to the radio station, she detailed her life and learning from her father the methods of staying warm and functioning in extreme cold. Her aging parents decided to buy a small house in Fairbanks, returning to the cabin in summer. This woman fascinated me, craving to know such a hardy person and experienced musher and trapper. I'm unsure I could perform as she has described her life. Trapping is hard work.

    Loading catches and long, dark trails lighted only by a head lamp, traveling alone on cold winter nights, returning to the cabin to skin and stretch pelts, back out again in a few days to check the traps again. What kind of woman can this be? Nothing like any woman I've ever known, nor man either. In her biographical letter to the radio station, she stated this was the only life she knew and made her living running her traps. I listened intently as the broadcaster read her letter. Her name was Angel and the locals called her the Arctic Angel. Everyone respected her.

Uncle Jake told me he wasn't feeling so good, weak, with a fever coming on. I feared it could manifest into pneumonia and told him, I thought I should take him to Fairbanks, as a precautionary measure. He agreed and I used my snowshoes to hike to Philo's cabin to inform him I was taking Uncle Jake to Fairbanks and to get Queenie, who was staying at Philo's cabin.

Philo returned to my cabin with Queenie and assisted me, harnessing the team and loading Uncle Jake. He did not show signs of deterioration but I didn't want to risk staying at the cabin while weather was good for travel. If a big storm came in, I could never get him to Fairbanks. I knew I had to make the run now. The trail was simple and we passed a small relief cabin at the half waypoint and those using the cabin always left a supply of firewood near the stove, just in case travelers like us would have difficulty.

We departed at 8 o'clock in the morning on the trail to Fairbanks, hoping to arrive in six hours. The trail was dark but my headlamp did a good job. Wolves see much better in the dark than humans and they showed no hesitation running at speed with an occasional bark, but mostly silence, broken only by sound of the sled's runners sliding on the snow, with the bright moon. Uncle Jake remarked he was okay, wrapped in furs. It was an indescribable emotion flying down that dark, lonely trail, emitting a spiritual sensation. It takes a certain mental strength and physical toughness to live and function in the arctic and no matter to what level I developed, I could never compare to my wolves. Queenie and her brothers were in their element, and from a personal perspective, I believe they are the grandest creatures ever to grace our planet. As Uncle Jake so profoundly stated, "They are magnificent."

We arrived at Fairbanks shortly after 2 o'clock in the afternoon. Many living outside Fairbanks in the surrounding area, use dog teams to go to town for various reasons and Fairbanks maintains sled paths to access different sections of town. The hospital was near where we entered town and I drove the team directly to the hospital, staking them in a designated area. I helped Uncle Jake to the emergency room door, although he didn't really need much help. He's a tough old guy and even with a high temperature, he was determined to walk the best he could by himself. They took him into an examining room to evaluate his condition. The doctor soon came out and said, "You did the right thing. His blood shows infection but I feel it has not spread significantly and should respond to IV drip using high dosage antibiotics. His temperature is above normal, though not in the danger zone but very likely would soon be at that point. We must keep him for at least a week to make certain he is gaining ground. Pneumonia is always a concern for folks his age with this degree of infection. I feel he will recover with the proper treatment.

"Are you staying nearby, so I can call you?"

"Yes, I'll stay at a friend's house." I gave Bill Foster's phone number to the doctor.

"Good, I'll call you as changes occur."

I called Bill and explained things. He asked if I wanted him to pick me up. I said I had my wolf team and he answered, "It is an easy trail to my house and you can stake the wolves in the backyard."

I was relieved to talk with Bill, inasmuch as he was very concerned about Uncle Jake. I told him we could visit Uncle Jake tomorrow at the hospital. I then took the team to Bill and Margaret's house. As I arrived, they greeted me in their always-delightful manner and were completely taken with my team. Of course, Queenie stole the show, as I expected.

I fed and watered the team and staked each one. They dig into the snow and form a shelter for themselves, withstanding any temperature in this manner.

Margaret made a magnificent dinner and we were filled with questions. I enjoyed explaining it all, giving me equal joy as we savored our opportunity to share this time. I told them I might need to stay a week to make sure Uncle Jake has recovered enough for travel. They were supportive to the maximum to help Uncle Jake and me in any way they could. They don't come any better than these two.

"I need to ask you two something that has been on my mind. I listened to Uncle Jake's radio, the station that periodically broadcasts news relating to those that live in the backcountry and the broadcaster spoke about a woman who runs her own trap line on the Tanana River. She was raised in a cabin and taught by her father since she was a child to trap fur for a living. They call her the Arctic Angel. Do you know about her?"

Bill said, "Of course, everyone knows of her, she's legendary, but we have never met her. She participated in the Tanana River 100 mile dog sled race two winters ago. Her dogs are freight dogs and not fast like the racers but she still finished third, which is remarkable. She's the real deal, as tough as any musher in Alaska and treats her dogs like her kids, unlike many serious racing mushers. I know she comes to Fairbanks to pick up supplies. Maybe we can find out when she makes these trips and meet up with her. She would go nuts over your wolf team. What fun that would be."

The next day, Bill and I visited Uncle Jake at the hospital. We talked to the doctor and he said Uncle Jake improved substantially but wanted him to remain in the hospital for a week as insurance the infection is gone. Even though he feels good, he's vulnerable at this stage.

Uncle Jake offered, "I'm ready to get out of this place, but the doctor, as he said, is insistent I stay to make certain all the infection is gone."

Bill replied, "Jake, we'll be here to visit you every day and I don't want you to rush your recovery."

"Okay, it'll give Samuel a chance to enjoy yours and Margaret's company. I'll stay here and pretend to be a good patient."

Queenie

Bill and I returned to his house and talked more about Arctic Angel. Bill said he thinks he knows the store where she buys supplies and he will ask the owner if he knows when she makes her trips. Bill called the storeowner later that day and asked him if Angel was scheduled to buy supplies. He reported to Bill she has no set schedule but is due in and may show up this week. Bill explained about my wolf team telling him I want to meet and talk with her. The storeowner wrote down Bill's number and said he would call when Angel shows up. I was enthusiastic about meeting Angel.

We visited Uncle Jake each day and the doctor said he is progressing to the good and a decision on his release should come sometime next week. He's eating well and feels good but until all traces of infection are gone he must remain on antibiotics. I felt relieved at this point.

The next day the storekeeper called Bill and said Angel just arrived with her dog team, is staking them and shortly will come into the store. She will stay awhile and talk to people, often eating at the store's lunch counter. Bill and I then headed to the store. As we arrived, a dog team was staked near the store, eight magnificent looking huskies. The sled had a rifle in a scabbard mounted on the side of the sled also displaying a graphic of an angel.

We went into the store and a small woman in a fur parka was talking to the storekeeper. We approached and the storekeeper knew Bill well and immediately introduced him to Angel Mackenzie and Bill introduced me to the storekeeper and Angel. My God, what a beauty and she shook my hand with a huge smile.

She voiced, "So nice to meet both of you. Art's been talking about you and telling me about Samuel's wolf sled team. I love wolves and my lead dog Sally Ann is one quarter wolf."

I was somewhat dumbstruck, but did manage a reply; "Angel, I am thrilled to meet you. I listened to a radio broadcaster explain your life and I am impressed. Can Bill and I buy your lunch today?"

"I normally would accept your offer and typically I do eat my lunch here but I am running late and my parents are expecting me. I always stay with them one or two nights when I come for supplies. They have a place where I can stake my dogs and my Mom and Dad enjoy preparing meals and our discussions. I suggest we all meet at my parent's house for dinner. I will call them from here. They are extremely social and to meet you two would be a delight for them and my Dad will go crazy when he finds out you have an all wolf sled team. He loves wolves and had many crossbred wolves during his years on the trails."

I gladly responded, "What a wonderful opportunity for all of us, Angel. Bill was a placer miner for years near my Uncle Jake's claim, now lives in Fairbanks like your parents. He has a wonderful wife Margaret. Would it be alright if Margaret comes too?"

"Of course, they will be honored. I will give you directions to their house."

I yearned to extend the conversation, with a long list of questions for Angel. Then I decided it would be impolite. Bill wrote down directions and we told Angel we would definitely be at her parent's house for dinner. She said seven is a good time. We stayed awhile to help Angel load supplies then she stood on her sled and commanded her huskies.

"Mush, hike, hike." Off they went and what a thrill it was.

Bill found the house and Angel's huskies were staked at the rear of the property. The houses were spread out, not a typical development. It was a modest frame house with a nice porch. Angel greeted us at the door and introduced us to her parents, Hubert and Mary Mackenzie. Mary was a native Alaskan Indian with long dark, graying hair immediately displaying where Angel inherited her traits, especially her amazing smile. Hubert was tall and fit looking for his age; I judged them to be in their mid-sixties.

Mary said, "How nice of Angel to invite you all to dinner. We enjoy company of those who share a similar life we have experienced. This rarely happens, especially since we moved to Fairbanks. Please sit down and I will serve tea and we can talk awhile."

Hubert said, "Angel told me about the wolf sled team. I must see these magnificent sled wolves. I knew one other, years ago, with an all wolf team. They were the best I have ever known in all my years in the arctic. You are most fortunate."

Mary said, "Dinner is nearly ready but we have time to talk." serving tea.

Hubert told their history, "Mary and I were married in 1930 and we worked together and built our cabin in 1935. I was born and raised in Minnesota. My uncle and brother were fur trappers and I learned the craft from them while growing up. They had a dog team and I was running the team from their tapper's cabin when I was fifteen years old and have lived life as a fur trapper since then. Angel was born in 1936 at our cabin. I delivered her, with Mary doing most of the work; it was an easy birth, for which I have been forever grateful. Angel was riding my sled checking traps when she was twelve. I bought her a team of huskies and a sled. She began her own trap line at 14. She's a natural outdoors person, probably inherited her mom's native genes, at least to some degree."

Bill remarked, "Margaret and I were at the start of the Tanana River sled dog race two years ago when Angel participated. She finished third among the best mushers Alaska has to offer. I learned of her abilities from that event."

"I was so proud of her," Hubert added. I know most of those champion mushers and believe me they knew they had a competitor on their hands when Angel entered the race. She may be small, but a tougher woman has never lived and I don't know of anyone that bonds with their dogs to Angel's degree, it's amazing to watch her interact with those huskies. They are dedicated to her.

"She finished third and her dogs are freight dogs, bred for power over speed, adding to her accomplishment. Her fellow racers were impressed and came up to her after the race and congratulated her."

Angel said, "My parents are responsible for not only giving me life, they have been my teachers in every manner of living. I have frequently thought how my life evolved, bringing me to this place in time. I'm twenty-three now and living in the arctic is all I know, a great advantage over someone coming from a less challenging place. All planetary life forms conform to their environment, or they perish. The trick for assimilation to the arctic environment is to understand it, adjust to it and not attempt to adjust it to personal comfort needs. It won't work, it's too foreboding. My Dad taught me about survival and how to be properly equipped to face any circumstance. He taught me how always to use extreme caution when on the winter trail alone. He taught me how to shoot my .300 Winchester as a protection against a rouge grizzly, which saved my life once. He taught me how to select and use the proper clothing and winter sleeping bag and how one can be comfortable at the most extreme temperature. It's where I am now and, also, who I am and think I will never leave the arctic. I have learned about solitude and how to cope with being alone in a wilderness for long spans of time. It's odd to hear many mention this. It's beyond their scope of thought how one can live alone in such a harsh place. How many people in New York City feel the sting of loneliness to a greater degree than I do in my cabin with my special and loving dogs? We, here, conquer loneliness through mental adjustment. Hundreds, of trappers and miners live in this region and many have lived alone for years."

Our meal was exquisite and Bill and Margaret were especially impressed. Margaret said, "I propose that tomorrow evening you three come to our house for dinner. This is so much fun, talking about the things we share and that have impacted our lives. Samuel can show off his wolf team and we can repeat our fellowship. One of Bill's friends gave us a large quantity of moose meat. I will make moose stroganoff, which everyone raves about. The trick to this dish is marinating and I will start this tonight. Angel will fall in love with Queenie, just as we all have. She is such a grand wolf."

We all agreed. I was excited to show my team to three people that know far more about dog sledding than I do, my being a true novice, but share their emotions for the trail and can only imagine the miles Hubert, Mary and Angel have logged on winter trails.

We stayed late talking about everything. Angel is so beautiful, with her long black hair and dark complexion. She's also articulate with an excellent vocabulary. I asked her about her education.

Replying, she said, "My parents schooled me. I have never attended school. Mom has a degree in English from the University of Alaska and Dad quit school in tenth grade, said he hated it, but has always been a reader from Mom's influence. I enjoy reading and we spent many hours reading hundreds of books on a variety of subjects, discussed them and we all learned from this sharing. Mom loves poetry and we read poems aloud to each other. I also love poetry but didn't at first, and it slowly grew on me. Now I write poetry. Reading and writing are good methods for coping with loneliness."

We departed, agreeing to repeat this event again at 7 o'clock tomorrow evening at Bill and Margaret's. In the morning, Bill and I will visit Uncle Jake to check his progress.

As we entered the hospital the doctor greeted us.

He said, "Samuel, your uncle is progressing well and I'm predicting another week and he will be fit for the trip back to the cabin. It's all he talks about."

"That's great news. We'll be here each day until he his released. Doctor, do you think it would be OK if Uncle Jake visited Bill's house for dinner tonight?

"No, he must remain here. He still shows infection in his blood and we simply cannot take the risk. He must be completely clear of infection before he can tolerate cold temperatures. I'm sorry but it's too risky."

We went to Uncle Jake's room and he was up and around and drinking coffee. I explained our experience, meeting Angel Mackenzie and having dinner with her at her parent's house.

He said, " I know who she is, everyone around here knows about her life and her talent handling sled dogs. She's an amazing young woman."

Bill and I returned to his house and I tended to my wolf team, fed and watered them. They seemed fine and happy as always. Wolves and dogs adapt quickly to most situations.

Just before seven, Angel and her parents arrived. The first thing they wanted was to see the wolf team. All three are lifelong mushers, which enhanced their interest. We went behind the house where the team was staked and they began a chorus of barking and whining at the sight of new friends.

Angel looked at me and said, "Samuel, they're the most magnificent team I have ever seen. Which one is Queenie?"

I challenged her, "Walk closer and see if you can identify her."

As Angel patted each wolf, the smile on her face said it all. Then Queenie rose on her hind legs and whined, waving her front feet in the air.

Angel looked at me and asked, "Is that her?"

"It sure is."

Then she stated, "Is she ever something special."

I offered the following, "She did something on the trail while I was bringing Uncle Jake to the hospital that surprised me. I noticed as we approached any kind of sharp turn or cross trail, just prior to getting the turn, Queenie would look back at me. I tried an experiment. When I'd give her the verbal direction command, I'd simultaneously raise my arm, either right or left. After we performed this a few times, I tried the hand signal only and Queenie immediately responded. I couldn't believe it. Have you ever seen or heard of this in your experience with your dog teams?"

"No, never have. It may have occurred but I have never heard of it. Dogs and wolves often only need a nudge to pick up new things and this is of no surprise but reflects the depth Queenie possesses. How fortunate you are to have her as your leader."

The evening was a repeat of the previous night. Mary complimented Margaret on her delicious moose stroganoff and Margaret told Mary she would give her the recipe. This dish melted in our mouths and had a distinct but indescribable flavor.

I asked Angel if she would accompany us to the hospital the next day to meet Uncle Jake. She said she would be delighted. I don't think I could ever get enough of Angel's company. Her beauty extends beyond the surface and never in my life will I again meet a woman like Angel. I knew that.

Bill said, "Samuel, take my car and you and Angel visit Jake. After your visit, you can take Angel to lunch. I insist."

"Thanks, Bill, I'd really enjoy that."

The next day Angel and I visited Uncle Jake. He was so joyful to see her and talk with her.

"Angel", he said, "I have known about you and your life for years. It seems a miracle you met Samuel. He listened intently to the Fairbanks broadcaster as he read your autobiographical letter. I am so happy to meet you.

"I should be out of here in another week and get back to our cabin. I sure do miss that place."

Angel said, "I am pleased you and Samuel know of my life. It came from circumstances and guidance of my incredible parents. They remain as my towers of strength and I look forward to visits when I come to Fairbanks for supplies. As you know, living alone in the arctic is mentally and physically challenging.

"People I meet for the first time and learn about my living design are astonished a small woman can live in this manner, because they lack relationship to the learning curve associated with my formative years. Native women performed similarly to my life for thousands of years, enduring hardships associated with arctic life. I align with those native women, as if their spirit lives inside me."

Angel captivated Uncle Jake. We talked about sled dogs and Uncle Jake told Angel the story of my rescuing the wolves when wolf bounty hunters caused the litter to be abandoned by poisoning their parents and older siblings. He also told her how he had studied this wolf pack for years, enjoyed observing their activity and felt certain a litter would be found in their den. Indeed, all six were rescued and they are now my sled team.

"I have observed wolves from my early years and my Dad has always enjoyed wolves. Sled dogs often are genetically linked to wolf ancestry," Angel said.

"Angel, you made a great showing last year in the Tanana River sled dog race," Uncle Jake said.

Queenie

"I have great respect for those racers, especially Bob Henderson and Ted Bishop, those guys are dedicated to racing and do a great job training their dogs. They use wolf crossbreeds mostly and those dogs a really fast. My dogs are not slow, but bred for strength more than speed and were not fast enough to catch those racers. I was happy to finish third, and hugged each dog at the finish line. I may try again this year, the race is a month away. I need to decide soon," Angel said.

"Angel, you can use my wolves this year. It's a six-dog team race and my wolves are very fast," I said.

Uncle Jake replied, "How perfect is that? You can visit our claim for a week or so and work with the wolves every day, until near race time. Samuel and I will be your support team. You can bring your team to our cabin and take both teams to Fairbanks for the start of the race. Samuel and I can stay with Bill and Margaret and you can stay with your parents until the start of the race. My God, would that ever be fun. You won't believe Queenie, she's the best lead dog I've ever seen and her harness mate, Incognito, is as fast as any of those other racer's dogs. He sets the pace as the rest of the team try to match his speed. I'll be out of here soon and we can activate this plan. Let's do it."

Angel said, "It's sure exciting to think about. I'm willing to try it. Queenie and her brothers are one of a kind. How can I ever refuse?"

Samuel said, "Angel, we must do it. It's too adventurous not to. Can you imagine the stir it will cause when you appear at the starting line with a team of wolves?"

A week later, Uncle Jake was out of the hospital and stayed with Bill and Margaret for two nights while everyone discussed the plan for Angel to compete in the Tanana River race. We discussed details and our group committed to work as a unit to support Angel. We'll all be at the starting line and also at the finish line. Hubert has a six passenger jeep and we'll crowd in and drive to the finish line to greet her.

We took both teams, Uncle Jake riding on my sled and headed toward the claim. At the half-waypoint, I switched with Angel and she drove my wolves the remainder of the distance. The weather was good, the trail was fast and we made the trip in less than six hours. The wolves displayed excitement as we neared home and the place sure looked good to Uncle Jake and me.

The wolves and Angel's dogs got along and they seemed to enjoy their new friendship. Angel staked out her dogs and the wolves went into their kennel, except Queenie; she took off at full speed toward Philo's cabin.

Angel asked, "Where is Queenie going?"

I told her about her bond with Philo, and she smiled, saying, "I must meet Philo."

I assured her, "You will soon. He'll come right away, after he greets Queenie. She has reversed his life to the good. It's quite a story. Philo's life was a mess; his cabin in complete disorder and alcohol ruled his life.

Queenie

Then he met Queenie. The cabin is now in perfect order and the booze is gone forever. She stays at his cabin."

Shortly, Philo appeared on snowshoes, heading our way with Queenie bounding ahead, barking as she arrived.

Angel smiled, "Isn't that something. Queenie never ceases to amaze me."

I introduced Philo to Angel and Philo smiled in awe. I told Philo she'd be driving the wolves in the upcoming Tanana River dogsled race.

He said to Angel, "You couldn't possibly have a better team; they have all the ingredients ... smart, fast and with great endurance. I helped Samuel and Jake train them to harness."

Uncle Jake put on his best display as a chef and made a moose steak with sourdough biscuits and brown gravy. The discussion centered on Angel, her life as a trapper and her childhood living in the cabin with her parents, learning all phases of arctic life.

"Angel, we can begin tomorrow allowing you to drive the wolves on area trails. I will follow with your team, and see how things develop," I interjected.

"I like the idea. It will be fun. I can't wait."

We talked late and then Philo and Queenie returned to their cabin. Uncle Jake retired to his room.

"Angel", I said, "I'll sleep here by the stove and you can sleep in the loft, which is warm and comfortable. That way, I can keep the fire going."

"Samuel, I don't want you to sleep by the fire, I want you to sleep in the loft with me. You and I share an emotional bond and it makes no sense for you to sleep on the cold floor. I am comfortable with you. How many times in one's lifetime do they feel true compatibility? Besides, we will be much warmer."

I was unsure how to respond. Angel is kind, with a depth of compassion seldom encountered.

"Angel, you are so beautiful and I am in love with you. I've never felt such love for a woman; I had a terrible childhood then I was trapped in a senseless war. I could never have imagined meeting someone of your beauty and character. Just being near you is pure ecstasy. You are right, we can keep each other warm and comfortable. That'll be perfect."

I was up first, stoked the fire and made coffee, then sat next to the stove, savoring the moment as thoughts of Angel dominated, contemplating my good fortune. It seems beyond comprehension. Angel came down the ladder and joined me.

"Well, Samuel," she said, without being coquettish, "how do you feel this morning?"

"I can't describe it. I never felt this way in my entire life. I love you so much. I'm so excited to help you with your race preparation. You'll enjoy driving this wolf team. Queenie and her brothers will charm you as they did me."

"I love you too, Samuel. I felt it from our first meeting at Art's store. I've lived isolated for such a large portion of my life, social interaction was minimal. I became attached to a fellow trapper several years ago, but alcohol dominated his life. It controlled him and he was drunk most of the time, and it became clear this is an unrealistic relationship and I moved on. I have two male sled dog friends, but with no physical chemistry and they are both married. Samuel, I just enjoy being with you, and now we are moving forward, beginning with this upcoming race. We share a passion for life and it feels good," Angel said.

Uncle Jake came in, looking for coffee. We began discussing practice runs.

"A good trail runs north along the creek for about ten miles. It's flat and easy running. I used this trail hundreds of times and, in a few places, it's better to move off the trail onto the creek itself. It's frozen solid now and creates a fast, smooth running surface," Uncle Jake said.

After breakfast, Angel and I harnessed our teams. Her dogs were wonderful. Samson was the largest and strongest, he ran in the "wheel" position and Sally Ann was the leader. Before Angel began to harness the wolves, she took a few minutes and talked with each wolf, calling them by name and further enhancing her bond with the team. She continued talking and petting them as she attached the harnesses. The wolves were enjoying this special attention. I told Angel to take the lead since the trail is easily identified and I'd follow. Off we went and what a feeling it was. Musher's all share emotions felt while driving dog teams on a beautiful trail.

We kept the pace slow and moved along the creek trail. About three miles down the trail, the creek widened and the trail became a little bumpy. Angel found an opening to enter onto the creek. She commanded Queenie with voice and arm signal to turn left onto flat surface of the the creek's. Then the most amazing thing happened. Queenie stopped, sat down and wouldn't move. I was right behind Angel, stopped and ran forward.

"Angel, she's never done anything like this before. She's always responded instantly."

I moved forward, scolding Queenie as she looked directly into my eyes. I felt something was bothering her.

Angel said, "Listen, I hear the sound of running water."

Exactly where the trail entered onto the creek, there was an air pocket with only a light ice coating. We could barely hear the water flowing, just beneath this thin ice.

I looked at Angel and she remarked without hesitation, "It appears to me that Queenie may have saved my life and the life of her brothers. If we had ventured onto the creek at this spot, the entire team, including myself, would have been in frigid water instantly and in their harnesses they would be unable to swim. This is the most amazing experience I have ever had. Queenie knew exactly what she was doing. Wolves hear about one hundred times better than humans; she heard the water and stopped in her tracks. Can you believe this girl?"

Queenie

Angel hugged Queenie, saying, "good girl, good girl". We were both shaken and gratitude for this wolf overwhelmed us. We continued on the trail staying off the creek entirely. We looped back toward the cabin and Angel stopped to talk.

"Samuel, I want to let the wolves run, get a feel for their speed potential."

"OK, good idea. I'll follow the best I can."

Queenie sensed it, and Angel called out. "Mush, hike, hike". Off they went, six stampeding wolves, they were flying down trail and Angel's huskies could not keep up. I was so thrilled and knew Angel was also.

When I arrived at the cabin, Angel was petting and congratulating each of her wolves and they were eating it up, tails wagging and barking with delight. Angel looked at me with her signature smile.

"My God, they are something to behold. The only way I cannot win the race would come from my own mistake along the course. My competitors cannot possibly keep up with this group. My strategy for the race is to let Henderson and Bishop set the pace. They are the two best racers with the best dogs. I will keep them in sight and then slowly let the wolves run. If I hold them back they'll maintain stamina for the finish line. Henderson and Bishop are friends and we watch out for each other regarding safety on the trail. They'll be well aware of my presence, following them."

We repeated our practice runs for three days. Then Angel decided she needed to return to check on her cabin. She would stop at Fairbanks and spend a night with her parents and leave for her cabin the next day. The race is two weeks away and we made a date to meet at Fairbanks a few days before the race. Angel's parents and Bill, Margaret, Uncle Jake and I will be at the starting line and, also, at the finish line. Anticipation was building as race day approached.

Flags and banners were everywhere promoting the Tanana River Race. I brought the wolves a day early with Uncle Jake. Angel had already arrived. I staked the wolves at Bill and Margaret's and we had dinner at Hubert and Mary's house. The air brimmed with excitement. Uncle Jake was more talkative than normal and enjoyed meeting Hubert and Mary. He knew of them but they'd never met.

Angel loaded her sled with an emergency tent, food and sleeping bag and carefully harnessed the wolves, constantly talking to them as she worked. She was remarkable with the wolves; they bonded further with her, which is very important to racing.

Angel took her team to the starting line. Twenty teams entered the race. The prize money was five thousand dollars for first place, adding interest to the race and bringing more competitors than usual. She greeted Henderson and Bishop and they talked for a while. These two men were hardened trail veterans and I felt comfort knowing they would be near Angel during the race. The wolves impressed both mushers and each had several crossbred wolves on their teams.

Queenie

The teams left at one-minute intervals with Henderson, Bishop and Angel the first three teams out, their positions based on performance in the previous Tanana River Race. We squeezed into Hubert's Jeep station wagon and headed for the finish line one hundred miles downriver at the small village of Backwater. All mushers were prepared for any and all conditions and will use powerful headlamps in darkness. The race finish will be in the dark. The fastest teams will cover the course in around ten hours.

Spectators had a big bonfire going and we huddled around this fire to wait for the arrival of the racers. Hubert had his binoculars and as time neared for arrival he scanned the landscape looking for his daughter. Then, in the distant darkness, we could see a light heading our way. Only one light, indicating this team was far in the lead. As the light grew brighter, Hubert's eyes were glued to his binoculars in and attempt to identify the team. He pulled his binoculars from his eyes and yelled out, "It's my Angel and she's really moving, probably thinking about that bonfire. That's my girl and she's a champion if there ever was one. My God, this is exciting."

Then we all began to cheer for Angel, it was a magical/angelic moment. A penetrating sensation to see this small woman with her wolves tearing through the snow and the team was running full out, with Queenie and her lead mate, Incognito, setting the pace. It was overwhelming and indescribable. That petite dynamo drove those wolves full speed breaking the finish line ribbon and receiving the checkered flag and she waved with both hands over her head, showing her magnificent smile. After she stopped, the first thing she did was hug each member of her team, praising them one by one. I walked over and hugged my Angel and could barely hold back tears. She looked magnificent and probably happier than any time in her life, as it was with me too. I have no memory of feeling such joy as I did that moment.

She gasped, "Samuel, it was really something. I must tell you it all."

Angel then fed and watered her team and I helped her stake them and they all made a place in the snow to lie down. Then we joined the cheering section and Hubert handed Angel a large cup of hot coffee, which she surely needed. Bill, Margaret and Mary were equally enjoying this eventful moment. Hubert was beside himself, so happy his daughter fulfilled her dream.

He said, "Angel, I could not possibly be prouder of you."

"Well, Dad, you did it, years ago, when you began training me in the ways of the arctic and how to run dogs and now wolves. It was amazing."

"Angel, please tell us about the race," I asked.

"It was quite trip. As predicted, it was a three-team race. I kept my pace down early, keeping Bishop and Henderson in sight. Henderson was pulling ahead some but I stayed fairly close to Bishop; stayed put until about the forty-mile mark and then passed Bishop. He gave me the thumbs up sign as I passed. Henderson was quite a

Queenie

ways ahead but I could see him in the distance. I began gaining on him but still did not push my team. I could see he was increasing speed trying to open the gap between us; so, I pressed the team a bit more to match his speed. The wolves wanted to run and I let them go. The gap got narrower and narrower, inasmuch as Henderson was doing all he could to gain speed from his huskies. They were topped out. Henderson went around a turn and was briefly out of sight and when I came around the same turn his sled was on its side and Bob was trapped under the sled agonizing in pain. I stopped the team and quickly righted his sled. As he tried to crawl, I realized he had broken his leg in the fall. Not a compound fracture but I was sure it was broken because he was in such agony. I asked him if he could stand up and with my help, he could, but barely. I cut a 'Y' limb off a spruce tree and made a crutch, bandaged the leg with an ace bandage with sapling splints on each side to support the broken leg. He said he thought he could still control his team if he went slowly. I lashed the crutch to the sled making it more stable to help support his leg. Bob said, 'Angel, I'm so grateful you were behind me. I think I can make it and Bishop will be along soon, he can check on me and probably run with me to the finish. You get going, girl and win your race. You deserve it. I'm your friend and I'll give you a special cheer when I arrive at Backwater.' I hugged Henderson and told him I'd be waiting for him and Bishop to arrive. Then I left with my fabulous wolves and now, here I am with you.

We will wait for Henderson and Bishop. They won't be too long."

I said, "Angel, those wolves may be the fastest sled team in Alaska. You are my heroine and I love you so much."

Spectators crowded around Angel, congratulating her. Hubert gave Angel a sandwich and more coffee. Mary hugged her daughter and Bill and Margaret added their joyful praise for Angel's accomplishment. The entire scene was a grand time for everyone.

A spectator shouted out that two teams were coming in. It was Henderson and Bishop running side by side finishing in a tie for second place. Angel went to each musher and hugged and congratulated them.

Henderson said, "Angel, you must consider Queenie to breed with my dog Thor, my best husky. Can you imagine the litter those two would produce? Your helping me on the trail will never be forgotten. Bravo, musher, you are the best."

Bishop agreed with Henderson about breeding Queenie and they both committed to assist any way they could.

A local restaurant owner gave free box lunches to everyone. His small restaurant would never accommodate such a crowd. The race organizers awarded trophies to Angel, Henderson and Bishop and everyone cheered these three as they stood together near the bonfire. In the cold and dark, the light of celebration shined brightly. It was an arctic event, and all present were attached to the Arctic and Alaska.

Most race participants had kennel trucks to carry dogs and trailers to haul sleds. Backwater had one roadhouse with no vacancy but the owner allowed Angel and I to sleep in the lounge next to the woodstove and tomorrow I will drive the team and Angel will ride when we return to Fairbanks.

As we sat together that evening our bond felt at a peak, and we talked far into the night about this experience and thoughts of our future.

"Angel, I want us to get married and live together at my cabin. It will be perfect for us. You can give up trapping, we can breed Queenie and with her reputation mushers from all over will be interested in her off springs. You can also sell harness-trained dogs for a premium price. I'll continue to work the claim and help you also. Your parents can use your cabin in summer months as they do now. It's such a great idea."

"Samuel, I couldn't agree more. We must do this, it will unite us and we will certainly have much to do between dogs, wolves and placer mining. How about as soon as we get back to Fairbanks?"

"You have just made me the happiest man on earth."

The trail to Fairbanks had perfect weather and we didn't push our team, loping along, savoring the surrounding spectacle of The Northern Lights. I loved driving the wolves; they're in their element and Angel, in her rare position as a passenger, enjoyed the ride.

Hubert and Mary planned a celebration dinner and Uncle Jake, Bill and Margaret attended. We told them the news of our intension to get married and they beamed with joy.

Hubert contacted a local minister and the wedding took place the next day at Hubert and Mary's house. A pivotal point in our lives and it could not have felt more blissful.

Angel was an angel in every manner imaginable. Margaret took on the task of our wedding day celebration dinner. Conversation was about our plans and we told them we will be living at the claim and hoping Angel's parents continue to use their cabin in summer months. Hubert and Mary said they'd do this as long as their health permitted. Their best years were at the cabin they had built together.

Angel called Bob Henderson to tell him about our marriage and, also, told him our plan to breed and train racing sled dogs. Henderson was not only a great racer he bred and sold sled dogs, too. He had a quality operation with large kennel space and in addition he created a program for Fairbank's teens to learn about sled dogs with hands-on-applications driving dog teams. Angel offered him her team and sled to use as a training team for his teen program. She also suggested mating Thor with Queenie and he could choose one of the pups.

Queenie

He was delighted and happy about our marriage and told Angel he would pick up her dogs and sled tomorrow with his kennel truck and she was welcome to visit his facility at any time. Angel was sad to give up her team but this gift to Henderson was an opportunity for her dogs and also relieving her responsibility of them. She knew Henderson well and told me he'd take excellent care of her dogs.

We greeted Henderson the next day and helped load Angel's dogs. He told us he'd bring Thor by boat after break up and we can see how things go from that point. It was a good plan.

Angel told me, "After I get settled at the claim, we can take a separate trip to my cabin. I want you to see where I've lived my entire life. I can gather a few things I need. We'll stay overnight at my parents house then make the two day trip to the cabin."

"I'll enjoy seeing where you were raised," I added. You and Uncle Jake will ride on the sled tomorrow for our return to the claim then we will begin to organize our lives in a new direction."

It felt good to see the claim again. We unharnessed the team and Queenie took off at full speed toward Philo's cabin. Philo showed up, greeting us and congratulating Angel on her victory. It's nice having Philo around. Queenie turned his life in a better direction and he's much happier.

We put the wolves in their kennel and Uncle Jake began preparing our meal. During our meal, we discussed things in general.

Uncle Jake said, "I plan to stay here all summer but feel next winter I should go back to Fairbanks to the care center. I'll be better off and it's easier for me day to day. As much as I enjoy this place, it's the right thing for me at this time in my life."

"Uncle Jake," I said, "You've done well this winter. Let's wait and see how it goes then decide. Angel and I want to do what is best for you, overall. Bill and Margaret love your visits and if you return to Fairbanks. I think you three can benefit from this companionship. They are such grand people, as you know."

Winter was on the wane and Angel and I read aloud passages from various books. Angel was very literary, from her Mom's teachings. She loved poetry and we recited inspirational poems. We listened to the Fairbanks radio station and hunkered down until spring arrived. Angel and Uncle Jake teamed up on meal preparation, producing gourmet meals. We three had long conversations and Uncle Jake convinced Angel to pursue more dog team racing next winter.

Often my mind drifted back to my Korean War experiences. I expressed this to Angel and Uncle Jake, "During combat in Korea I felt despair beyond description. I was convinced I would be killed in the war. To project from that point to now is as if I died and transcended to heaven and woke up in paradise, living a dream life. I'm looking forward to summer, breeding Queenie and the excitement, seeing where this all leads. Wolves' average lifespan is eight years so they won't be with us too long. We must grasp all we can from the time given."

Spring arrived and as promised Henderson brought Thor, what a beautiful dog. The wolves accepted him completely. Henderson stayed one night and said he would retrieve Thor after the puppies arrive.

Queenie came into heat and we staked the other wolves, letting Thor and Queenie use the kennel. We watched them breed on several occasions then it became a wait and see situation. Angel knew how to determine when Queenie was pregnant. Queenie had eight puppies and it was such a sight. She took maternal care of these beauties and all of us were delighted to share her joy.

Philo came each day to check on his friend and watching him react to the puppies it's difficult to believe at one time he said he didn't care for dogs too much. What a change.

Angel and I took the boat with Thor to call Henderson, telling him he could pick him up at Bill and Margaret's house. He arrived and told us he will visit the claim after enough time passes for the puppies to be on solid food and pick his choice of the litter. We bought supplies and returned to the claim.

Angel was ecstatic with Queenie's puppies. They consumed her totally and she would get up in the middle of the night to check on them. Angel and Queenie became incredibly bonded, sharing this very special time.

As warm temperatures arrived, I resumed mining and Angel helped but she was also busy with her husky/wolf crossbreeds. Although too young for harness training, she'd take hikes with Queenie and her bundles of energy. They hiked daily to Philo's cabin and Queenie was always excited to see Philo. She had developed a desire to stay at our claim more now after she had her puppies.

Chapter 5 Loss

Winter arrived and Angel worked diligently with her young team. She entered the Tanana River race with her original six-wolf team and won the race by a wide margin. She told me she would retire the wolves from racing and put all her energy into training her crossbred huskies.

Major changes have occurred this winter. Angel and I are trying to adjust the best we can. Philo died in his sleep and I discovered him. I sat at his bedside and wept uncontrollably then summoned Angel and we shared the grief of Philo's passing. We loved Philo, and Queenie was confused, kept smelling his body and whining. Seeing Queenie react caused us to both of us to break down again. It was very painful to lose Philo; he was an attachment to all our lives. The wolves and I will take Philo's body to Fairbanks on the sled for cremation. Angel stayed behind to care for her dogs.

    The day of Philo's death, I sifted through his personal papers trying to find information about relatives. I remembered he told me he had no living relatives but I thought I might find someone but found none. In a small box was an envelope with "Jake or Samuel" written on it. Inside I found a letter and will, leaving his claim to Uncle Jake and me. The letter stated, "*I'm certain am dead now or you would not be reading this letter. I rather felt I would die at my claim. It's OK though, because this place has been wonderful to me and Jake and Samuel are my best and only friends in life. The will is legal, had it drawn up by a lawyer in Fairbanks, his name and number is on the will in case you need him for anything. Also, you will find a map where my gold stash is located. My guess it's about 100,000 dollars. It makes me feel good to give these things to you two. The saddest thing about my dying is losing Queenie, she was my savior and showed me clearly what love looks like and I loved her so very much. Queenie is really my only regret about dying. I'm plenty old to die but that girl melted my heart from the beginning and made my life so much better, looking forward to each new day. Take good care of my sweet friend; she is the best in the world. Philo Ketchum."*

Angel said, "We can't just keep crying and crying," and she burst into tears again.

Angel helped harness our six wolves and also helped load Philo's body. Queenie watched every move and I think she knew exactly what had happened. I had Philo cremated and saved his ashes. Uncle Jake was at the care center and I had to tell him about Philo. This was extremely difficult and the grief repeated itself.

Uncle Jake said, "What few realized about Philo is just how kind and thoughtful he really was. He said you and I were his best friends and we feel he was also our best friend. It rips my heart out to think of him as gone. Queenie recognized his character immediately. Animals sense these things, not sure what it is, but I have seen it before and I suspect it is chemically projected from the person, and animals detect this and react. I will now think and dream about Philo for many nights. I'm looking forward to summer and returning to the claim."

Uncle Jake never made it back to the claim. He had a heart attack the next month and died at the care center. Bill and Margaret held a memorial service for Uncle Jake as a celebration of his life. Over one hundred people attended—those he had come to know during his years in Alaska. Angel's parents assisted and served food to those who remained for Uncle Jake's wake. I found among his belongings his journal, documenting his years at his claim and Angel and I read it aloud over the next few weeks in our cabin. It was so amazing to read details about when he first came to Alaska and the struggles he endured to stake his claim and make it productive. Pictures' show him and Bill erecting the cabin's walls and showed his dog teams. One photo showed his hand full of gold nuggets, his first major discovery. He looked so young and vibrant.

Chapter 6 Moving Forward

The reality, most prominent allowing me to cope with this intense grief was the presence of Angel, my partner. I cannot imagine how I would ever gain back quality life without her.

Our life changed without Uncle Jake and Philo, and during the past few years we adjusted as the healing elixir of time worked its magic and our new direction revealed many rewards. We retired the wolves from harness but vowed to do all in our power to give them the life they deserve. We built a retirement kennel for our beloved wolves. Except Queenie and Incognito, they moved into the cabin. Those two shared many miles of trail side by side and Incognito had a special bond with Queenie, he added a comic, lighthearted element to Queenie's intellect. He made us laugh with his antics and prodded Queenie to play "chase me" when they were outside and they were both intensely attached to Angel, following her where ever she went in the vicinity of the claim.

In winter months, Angel took her team to nearby dogsled races, now a team of eight as a result of Queenie's second litter. Angel is now thirty but shows no loss of anything, even more beautiful and was the dominant sled dog racer in the territory, viewed with immense respect from all other racers. She volunteered to help Henderson teach his teen dog-racing program during its session. She wrote letters to congressmen and senators to encourage bounty removal on wolves, citing how environmental studies reveal wolves' benefit caribou and other animals of the forest serving as a balancing mechanism, as they have done for thousands of years.

I have decided to end this narrative describing my life at this point. As I interact each day with my aging and loving rescued wolves, my attachment to them is higher than it has ever been. I cannot possibly assign myself the task to record their declines and deaths. The intensity of pain losing those precious beings would be far too difficult. I want to live out my remaining years sharing each precious day and keeping fixed in my mind an indelible image of six beautiful, little life forms peeking over a rock in their den with curiosity wondering about this invader. I want to maintain my memory of carrying six bundles of fur down the hillside and Uncle Jake greeting me with his big smile. It was a pivotal point in my life and how wonderful it was. I now have an angel living with me in a heavenly place with indefinable grandeur and, as Angel and I sit near the wood stove on a cold winter's night with Queenie and Incognito, we four savor our time remaining and feel the joy brought forth from our love.

From Uncle Jake's journal, "*I came to this place as a young man, filled with energy and desire to experience an adventurous life. Alaska is like no other place, its dimension and ubiquitous mountains and rivers reach the horizon in every direction. It's a foreboding place, offering comfort only to those who understand it, merge and wend with it. All life here is interactive, a symbiosis afar from human created spaces designed for ease of living, often resulting in clashes, lacking ability to discover peaceful equilibrium. As I observe the wolf pack I see clearly how they have thrived so long in this harsh place. They epitomize order and unity in a progression of life. They are dependent on each other and recognize this as their engine. They are spiritually attached to Earth and its cosmic design and I feel they know this. May be the reason it's popular among them to howl at the moon.*

"As I sift the gravel each day for flakes of gold I feel as if the wolf is guiding me. Life has blessed me beyond description." Jake Glaser

About the Author

Raymond Greiner

He lived in Vienna, WV until 1951, moved to Marion, Ohio until 1957, attending Harding High School in Marion, Ohio moving to Utica, NY for his senior year of high school, graduating from Utica Free Academy public school in 1958. Greiner served four years in the USMC, honorably discharged in 1961. He attended Utica College and Wayne State University, married in 1964 to Nancy McClellan and raised three children. He started a restaurant and developed a consulting service as an advisor to investors. Retired at age 60, he is pursuing writing; he is a dedicated reader.

Made in the USA
Charleston, SC
08 September 2015